GET TO KNOW SY[L...]

Once a year, seals must spend extra time on land to shed their outer layer of hair (a process called molting).

A seal's pectoral (or fore) flippers are webbed with five bony digits.

A seal propels itself through the water by moving its hind flippers from side to side.

Andrea Reitmeyer

SYDNEY THE SEAL SAVES THE SEA

This is Sydney. Sydney is a young seal who lives in the North Sea. He has four fins, which help him swim very well. The sea is Sydney's playground.

Like most seals, Sydney often swims alone, but on land he likes to curl up with other seals. On the sand banks of the tideland, Sydney is protected from predators and can relax with his family.

One day, Sydney's peaceful family life was interrupted by a visit from a very different looking seal. Her snout was a bit longer. Her skin was a bit darker. She was like no other seal Sydney knew from the tideland.

The strange seal held a shiny red object in her flippers. Then she let it go and the water carried it closer to Sydney's family.

While his family inspected the object, Sydney swam up to the visitor.

"I'm Roberta," she told him. "I'm a grey seal, and I need your help. Will you follow me?"

Sydney didn't hesitate, and soon Roberta was leading him through algae forests and deep gorges.

Eventually the two seals came to a rocky landscape and Sydney was startled by what he saw.

"Look," Roberta whispered to him. "Someone has thrown away an old fishing net and a walrus is tangled in it."

Sydney quickly saw what must be done.

"We have to rescue it," he told Roberta, "together."

Roberta and Sydney got to work, pulling at the net with their teeth.

When the snares loosened, the walrus swam off—and so did Roberta. "Follow me," she said, swimming away.

As they continued, Sydney noticed a swarm of jellyfish, floating lifelessly in the water.

"They're actually plastic bags," Roberta explained. "They make sea creatures who prey on jellyfish sick."

Sydney's flippers were getting tired when Roberta stopped. They had reached Roberta's home—and Sydney couldn't believe what he saw.

Roberta's family was surrounded by discarded trash. Plastic bags, bottles, and even toys floated about.

Beneath the surface, things got even worse.

There was a huge pile of garbage. "Now you see why I swam to your family for help," Roberta explained. "If things don't change, your tideland will be covered in litter, too." Sydney worried that his family's help would not be enough. "We'll need all the animals," he insisted. "Every snout, fin, tooth, and pincer!"

Together, Sydney and Roberta gathered all the nearby sea creatures.

"The ocean is not a trash bin," Roberta began.

"It's our home," continued Sydney. "But the humans who make all this garbage don't live with it like we do. We have to bring the trash back to them so they can see what they've done."

It wasn't hard for the animals to find the humans. For, in spite of their polluting ways, they clearly loved the ocean. They sailed on its waves, fished on its shores, and played on its beaches.

"Plastic bottles, bags, and cans," grumbled one sailor. "Disposable things only make life easier until they pile up as trash. Maybe it's time we stop doing what's easy, and start doing what's best."

As the animals' mission became more widely known, people began pitching in. They helped clean up waste now, too.

People of all ages and backgrounds worked together to help free the sea and its beaches from waste.

Eventually, their part of the ocean was clean again—but Sydney worried that it wouldn't last.

"If humans truly love the sea," he told Roberta, "they'll have to stop making so many disposable things."

As Roberta glided through the clear and clean water again, she playfully splashed Sydney.
"I'm not giving up on these humans," she said. "Not yet."

REDUCE. REUSE. RECYCLE.

Humans can't rely on animals—like Sydney and Roberta to help us take better care of the Earth. People all around the world need to get involved and show that they care.

What can you, your friends, and your family do to make a difference? Start with the three Rs: reduce, reuse, and recycle.

REDUCE: *Reducing* means using less of something. For instance, many shops have stopped providing single-use plastic bags. Customers bring reusable ones with them instead to carry their items home. This *reduces* unnecessary plastic, which is helpful to everyone!

REUSE: Think about all the individual items you use and throw away in just one day. That's a lot of waste! Try incorporating reusable containers and items like the ones this chart suggests.

ITEM	DISPOSABLE	REUSABLE
1. Sandwich	baggie	sealed container
2. Drink	juice box or pouch	thermos
3. Napkin	paper	cloth
4. Utensils	plastic	metal

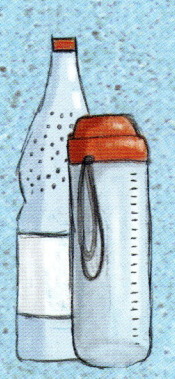 

RECYCLE: *Recycling* allows us to find new uses for otherwise disposable items. We often recycle paper, plastic, and glass. For example, daily newspapers can be made from recycled paper instead of brand-new. Unfortunately, a lot of trash that can't be recycled ends up in garbage dumps. As those pile up, trash becomes litter that pollutes the oceans upon which we depend.

Would you like to help protect the Earth's oceans from plastic? Learn more from sites like **oceana.org** and **oceanconcservancy.org**, and look for beach clean-up opportunities near you.

For Kilian & Emilie,
who love the sea as much as I do

Andrea Reitmeyer was born in East Friesland, Germany, and studied Communication Design at the Mainz University of Applied Sciences. As an illustrator and author, she has written many books about animals in her homeland of Germany, such as *Emily and the Sea; Emily, the Wind and the Waves; Emily on the Farm; Paul the Cat and the Red Thread; Elio Wants to be Great; I Dare You, Ida!; and Little Bee Hermine, What Is Your Home?* She lives with her family in Mainz, Germany.

Original title: Robin. Ein kleiner Seehund räumt auf (ISBN 978-3-8337-4010-7)
Illustrations and Text by Andrea Reitmeyer
Copyright © 2019 Jumbo Neue Medien & Verlag GmbH, Hamburg/Germany;
All rights reserved. No part of this book may be reproduced or transmitted in any form or by any means, electronic or mechanical, including photocopying, recording, or by any information storage and retrieval system, without permission in writing from the publisher.

First published in the United States of America in March 2020 by "Clever-Media-Group" LLC
www.clever-publishing.com

ISBN 978-1-951100-009-4 (hardcover)

For information about permission to reproduce selections from this book, write to:
Clever Publishing
79 Madison Avenue
8th Floor
New York, NY 10016

For general inquiries, contact:
info@clever-publishing.com

To place an order for Clever Publishing books, please contact The Quarto Group:
sales@quarto.com
Tel: (+1) 800-328-0590
Manufactured, printed, and assembled in China

10 9 8 7 6 5 4 3 2 1

LIFESPAN
Seals can live anywhere from 25 to 30 years long. Females usually live a couple years longer than males.

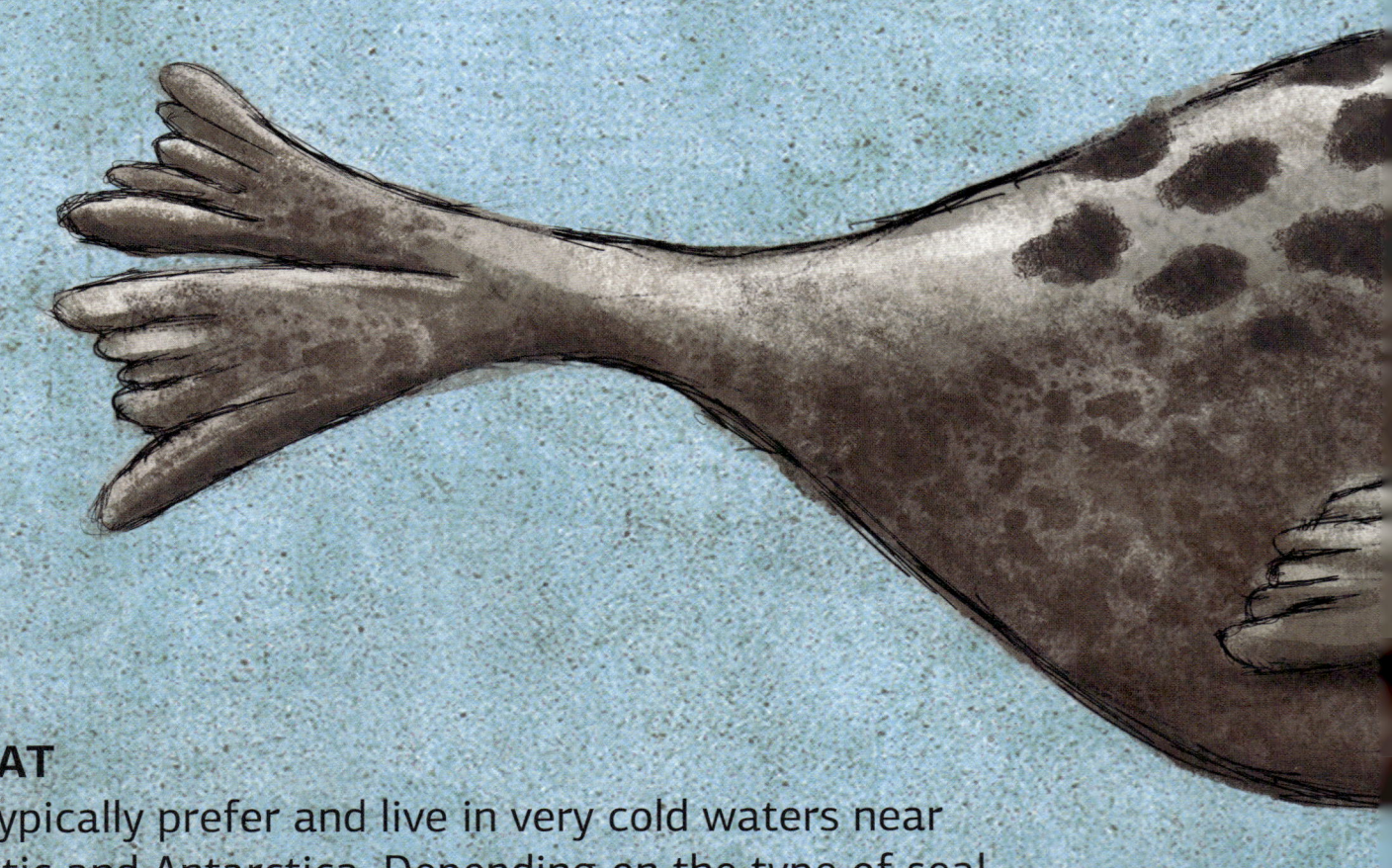

HABITAT
Seals typically prefer and live in very cold waters near the Arctic and Antarctica. Depending on the type of seal, though, they also live in the Northern Pacific (between Asia and North America) and off the coasts of South America, southwestern Africa, and southern Australia.